Having Fun

Then and Now

Lara Whitehead

NELSON
CENGAGE Learning™

Australia • Brazil • Japan • Korea • Mexico • Singapore • Spain • United Kingdom • United States

Having Fun, Then and Now

Text: Lara Whitehead
Design: Vonda Pestana
Editor: Liz Alger

Acknowledgements
The author and publisher would like to acknowledge
permission to reproduce material from the following
sources:
AAA Collection, p. 19B;AAP Image, p. 22 & bottom, p. 31
bottom left /Thomas Kienzle, p. 6 /POOL, p. 7 /Walt
Disney/Joan Marcus, p. 11 /Jeff Walker/Famous, p. 23 top
/Dean Lewis, p 23 bottom; Australian Picture
Library/Corbis/Michael Nicholson, back cover, p. 20
bottom /Adam Wollfitt, p. 13 top /Historical Picture
Achieve, p. 19D; Bridgeman Art Library/LaurosGiraudon,
pp.18 (Deck of Cards), 19E; Corbis, p. 20 top;photolibrary.
com, pp. 8, 13 bottom, 17, 18 (Dice, Checkers), pp. 26-27, 29
bottom, 31 top right; Picture Desk/ArtAchieve, p. 12 /Musee
du Lourve/Dagli Orti, p. 5 top /Egyptian Museum
Caior/Dagli Orti, p. 19C/National Museum Karachi/Dagli
Orti, p. 19F /Bettmannm pp. 24, 31 top left /Bargello
Museum Florence/Dagli Orti, p.30 bottoml Stock Photos,
pp. 4-5 bottom, 28 /Masterfile, front cover, p. 29 top.

PM Extras Non-Fiction
Ruby
Caring for the Earth
Changing Cultures
Having Fun, Then and Now
Change in the Community
Communities Everywhere
Past Work, Future Work

For product information and technology assistance,
in Australia call 1300 790 853;
in New Zealand call 0508 635 766

For permission to use material from this text or product,
please email **aust.permissions@cengage.com**

ISBN 978 0 17 011469 1
ISBN 978 0 17 011464 6 (set)

Cengage Learning Australia
Level 7, 80 Dorcas Street
South Melbourne, Victoria Australia 3205

Cengage Learning New Zealand
Unit 4B Rosedale Office Park
331 Rosedale Road, Albany, North Shore NZ 0632

For learning solutions, visit **cengage.com.au**

Printed in China by 1010 Printing International Ltd
5 6 7 8 9 13 12 11

Contents

Chapter 1

Sports

Playing and watching sports has been a form of entertainment for thousands of years. The ancient Greeks started the Olympic Games, while the Romans built huge stadiums to watch **chariot** races. Today, millions of people still play or watch sporting events for fun.

The ancient Olympics

Long ago, in 776 BC, the first ancient Olympic Games were held in Greece. They were part of a religious **festival** in honour of **Zeus**, the father of all the Greek gods and goddesses. The only event held in the very early Olympic Games was the foot race.

A modern stadium can hold hundreds of thousands of spectators.

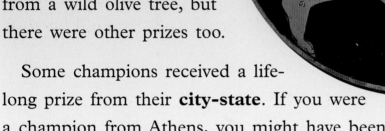
a painting of an ancient Greek discus thrower

The word **athlete** comes from an ancient Greek word that means 'one who competes for a prize'. At the ancient Olympic Games, the greatest prize for winners was a branch from a wild olive tree, but there were other prizes too.

Some champions received a life-long prize from their **city-state**. If you were a champion from Athens, you might have been awarded one free meal a day at the city hall for the rest of your life. Or, you might have been allowed to live free of charge in the **Pyrtaneum**, a special hall where important citizens lived. Other city-states allowed champions to stop paying taxes for four years. Other ancient prizes for Olympic champions included oxen, shields, woollen cloaks and olive oil.

The modern Olympics

Today, the Olympic Games include many different sports, such as beach volleyball, mountain biking, softball and trampolining. Millions of people around the world watch them on television. However, unlike athletes in the past, modern athletes compete for gold, silver and bronze medals.

Katharine Merry, Cathy Freeman and Lorraine Graham display their 400 metres medals at the 2000 Olympic Games.

The modern Olympics also include other forms of entertainment. Opening ceremonies – such as those at the 2000 Olympic Games in Sydney – blend music, dance and theatre. At the end of Sydney's opening ceremony, athlete Cathy Freeman lit the Olympic flame in a dramatic ending to the night's entertainment.

Cathy Freeman lighting the Olympic flame at the 2000 Olympic Games in Sydney.

Chapter 2

The London Times July 10, 159

❈THEATRE❈

Romeo & Juliet

a play by Shakespeare

Reviewed by Matthew Inkspot

Last night was the opening of a new play by William Shakespeare, called *Romeo and Juliet*. Romeo and Juliet fall in love, but their families hate each other. They refuse to allow the two young people to see each other. If you want to know how the story ends, come to the Globe Theatre this weekend.

Admit One
Romeo & Juliet
one penny

The best actor was the young boy who played Juliet. Since no women were allowed on stage, boys played all of the female parts. They looked quite lovely in their dresses and wigs!

Unfortunately, the special effects in the play were rather basic. Romeo carried a burning torch when it was supposed to be night time. Juliet's balcony was just a small platform above the stage. However, the words were so beautiful that I could still imagine Romeo in a lush garden, wooing Juliet on her stone balcony.

You can buy a ticket to the play for just one penny, but you'll have to stand on the dirt floor of the pit below the stage. Three pennies will get you to the Gentlemen's Room with a cushion for the hard wooden benches. Wealthy viewers might wish to pay more and sit in the upper levels of the theatre. When the trumpet blasts, be sure to quieten down so the play can begin.

Overall, I think *Romeo and Juliet* is a rather good play and worth the ticket price. Let's hope Shakespeare continues to write more plays in the future.

A review of
'The Lion King Musical'
by Josh, Grade 4

Last weekend I went to see The Lion King with my mum and dad. It was really great. The actors all wore huge masks and costumes so that they looked like animals, but still looked kind of human too. There were also lots of huge puppets, controlled by people inside (I think).

In the part when the wildebeests stampede, the special effects were awesome. It really looked and sounded as if thousands of crazy wildebeests were rushing straight at Simba, and me! The lights were flashing and the wildebeests seemed to be getting bigger and bigger. I know they were just pictures and puppets, but they really made me feel as if I was going to be flattened.

I'd say everyone who has the chance should go and see the show!

The stage

The basic design for theatres hasn't really changed since ancient times. But modern theatres do have some extra features, such as fancy lighting and staging equipment, comfortable seating, speaker systems and the orchestra pit.

This amphitheatre was built in Ostia during the time of the Roman Empire.

A curved seating plan, set on a slope, allows many people to see the entire stage at the same time.

This model shows how the theatre would have looked in 1599.

In Shakespeare's Globe Theatre, the cheapest tickets let you stand directly in front of the stage.

In modern theatres, seats directly in front of the stage are often the most expensive.

Chapter 3

Home

Snowed in at Grace's house

February 20, 1880

Dear Diary,

Today it snowed for the third day in a row. The snow was
deep for us to play outside. So we played together inside
Yesterday the Kellors came to visit in their sleigh and st
overnight. This morning, Klara and I cut out paper dolls
bits of newspaper. David and Eli played checkers. Then
jumped onto the board and knocked all of the pieces c
floor! One of the black pieces got lost. Father whittled
in the afternoon.

Mr Kellor also brought his **fiddle** and we sang toget
dinner cooked. After dinner we had a square dance! I
great fun!

Mr Kellor started off playing slowly while we practised. Then he began to play faster and faster, so we had to dance faster and faster. Afterwards we all laughed and flopped down by the fire to rest.

Father brought out the corn popper, and we ate popped corn while Mrs Kellor told us stories about her childhood. When she was a little girl, her family moved from Pennsylvania to Oregon in a covered wagon. I'd heard her story before, but I always like hearing it again.

Now it's time to blow out the lamp. I hope the snow will stop tomorrow so we can go sledding outside. Klara and I plan to make the biggest snowman ever!

Goodnight!

Grace

E-mail from Matthew

send   attach   addresses   options

To: ▼ Zara@z-girl.net.uk

Subject: Stuck inside

To: Zara in London
From: Matthew in Australia
Re: Stuck inside

Hi Zara,

We're having a heatwave and I'm stuck inside today. It's 43°C outside and Mum says we're staying out of the sun until after 3:00 at least. I've been playing computer games this morning, but I'm kind of sick of them now.

How are you doing, building your Robotron? I've got mine so he moves his head, but I can't make his arms move with the remote yet. I think one of the wires must be loose, but I can't work out which one. I'll e-mail you a video clip when I get him working.

save

Have you got your new digital camera yet? Send me a photo of the snow at your house. I could make it my screen saver and pretend it's cold in my house when I see it!

I've got to go and turn down the air conditioner. Mum will have a fit if she notices how cold I set it!

Talk to you soon,

Matthew

Mix and match

Today we have many types of games to play, but some of them were invented long ago. Can you match the old games to the new ones?

Jacks

Chess

Deck of cards

Cribbage

Dice

Checkers

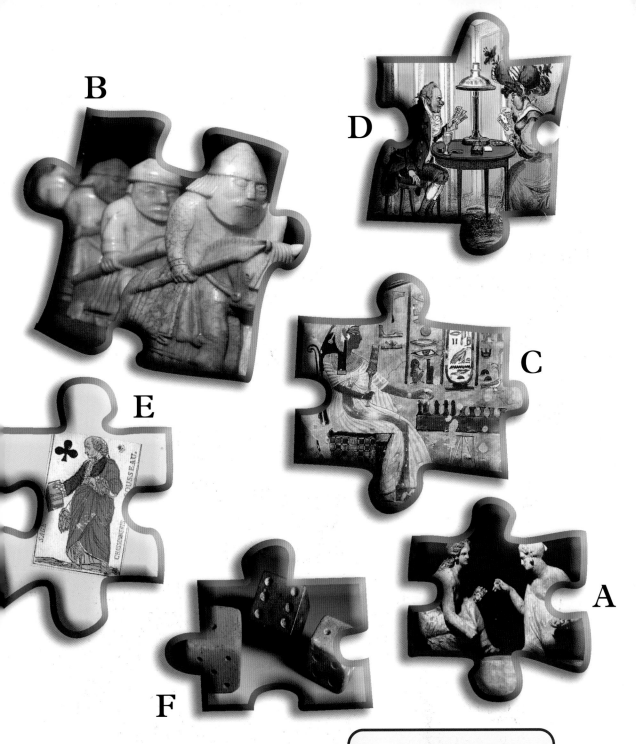

19

Chapter 4

Music

Minstrels

Around 800 years ago, wandering musicians called **minstrels** started travelling from town to town across Europe. They entertained peasants and kings, singing songs of love, war and brave deeds. They played instruments like the harp, the recorder and the lute.

Come One, Come All
to an
Evening's Entertainment
by
The Travelling Minstrels of Paris

Hear them sing their famous songs:

Hopeless Love for a Noble Lady

Searching, Searching for a Unicorn

And, winner of the French Court's

Most Popular Song of the Year,

She Loves Me, She Loves Me Not

One show only!

Also featuring juggling, acrobatics and magic!

See them tonight

at The Lute in Arms, Baker's Street.

The Beatles wave as they arrive at London airport, England.

Beatlemania!

In the early 1960s, a British band called The Beatles hit the charts with their song, *Love Me Do*. They soon became the most famous pop group in history. During their time together, The Beatles travelled to many countries to play their music.

People around the world could hear their songs on the radio, buy their record albums, go to concerts and even see them on TV or in the movies. For one of the first times in history, radio and TV allowed millions of people to enjoy the same music at the same time.

Atomic Kitten
live in concert

Today there are lots of music groups that are famous around the world. Their songs travel much more quickly these days. We can watch **webcasts** of concerts and listen to music on CDs and DVDs.

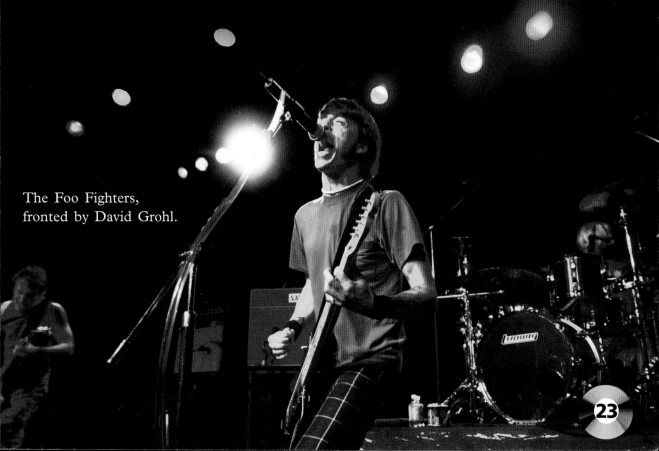

The Foo Fighters,
fronted by David Grohl.

Chapter 5

Machines

Riding high in the sky

Ferris wheels were invented more than a hundred years ago, but they have not changed very much in that time. The first Ferris wheel was built by a bridge builder named George Ferris. He designed his amusement ride for the Chicago World's Columbian Exposition of 1893. Four years earlier, the Paris Expo had built the Eiffel Tower. The Chicago Expo wanted something even bigger and better.

Interview with Mr George Ferris, inventor of the first Ferris wheel.

Reporter: What made you decide to build a giant wheel?

Mr Ferris: The Chicago Expo wanted something really amazing for people to come and see. I always thought that merry-go-rounds were fun, so I decided to build a huge one, only I turned it on its side. That's how I came up with my giant wheel idea.

Reporter: How big is your wheel?

Mr Ferris: It's 75 metres tall, and can hold 2,160 passengers. It's the biggest wheel in America today.

Reporter: How did you actually build the wheel?

Mr Ferris: We hired the Detroit Bridge and Iron Works to make the wheel. They were a little surprised when they saw the plans, though! They thought I was just nuts to build a wheel that big.

Reporter: And when the Expo is finished, what will happen to your wheel?

Mr Ferris: Well, it's just going to get cut up and sold for scrap metal. I don't think anyone will ever build one again. Too bad – I thought it was a fun idea.

Reporter: Umm, yes, that's a pity. Well, thanks for all that.

The London Eye

If you thought Ferris wheels were an old-fashioned ride, you should see the new London Eye! It's twice as tall as Mr Ferris' original wheel, and instead of swinging out in the cold air, you can ride inside a comfortable pod.

the **LONDON** eye

Opened	February 2000
Height	135 metres
Number of passengers	800
Number of pods	32, holding 25 people each
Time for one turn	30 minutes
Speed	30 cm per second
Architects	Julia Barfield and David Marks

Chapter 6

Changing Technology

Technology has changed the way we enjoy lots of types of entertainment, but it hasn't really changed the things we still like to do.

• Sports fans can watch slow-motion instant replays.

• Video replays also help sporting officials make calls during a game.

• CDs and DVDs mean we can listen to music in comfort, or on the move.

- The internet allows us to play computer games with people from around the world.

- Hand-held computer games mean we can take our entertainment with us.

- Musicals and plays on stage use computer lighting and lasers to add special effects to the show.

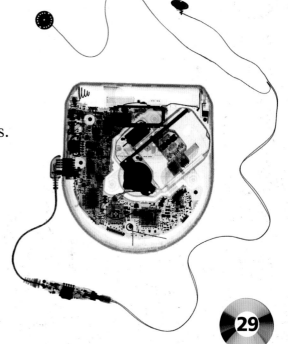

Chapter 7

Timeline

1400 BC
People start to play checkers.

1300
The first playing cards are mass produced in Europe.

776 BC
The first Olympic Games are held.

1600s
The rules for cribbage appear written down.

600 BC
First written mention of chess.

1200
Wandering musicians, called minstrels, appear in France.

Admit One
Romeo & Juliet
one penny

1592
Shakespeare writes *Romeo and Juliet*.

1893

First Ferris Wheel built at the World's Columbian Exposition of Chicago.

2000

The London Eye opens.

1980s

Music CDs become available.

1939

First television broadcasts are made.

1975

The home version of *Pong*, one of the first video games, is released.

1960s

The Beatles become popular.

1972

The first home VCR becomes available.

Glossary

athlete a person who competes in a sport

chariot a racing cart with two wheels, pulled by a horse

city-state a state made up of a city and its surrounding towns

festival a time of celebration

fiddle violin

minstrels wandering musicians in France

Pyrtaneum a special hall where important citizens lived

webcasts video recordings played over the Internet

Zeus the father of all the Greek gods and goddesses

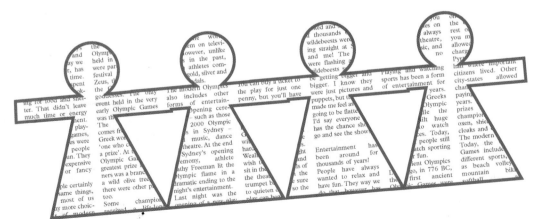